SIKSIKAITSITAPI

....

STORIES OF THE

BLACKFOOT PEOPLE

SIKSIKAITSITAPI

• • • •

STORIES OF THE
BLACKFOOT PEOPLE

PAYNE MANY GUNS, CRYSTAL MANY FINGERS
SHEENA POTTS, LATASHA CALF ROBE, TIM FOX
MARLENE YELLOW HORN, DerRic STARLIGHT

FOREWORD BY ALAYNA MANY GUNS

DURVILE &
UpRoute Books

Calgary, Alberta, Canada

Durvile & UpRoute Books
UPROUTE IMPRINT OF DURVILE PUBLICATIONS LTD.
Calgary, Alberta, Canada
Durvile.com

LIBRARY AND ARCHIVES CATALOGUING IN PUBLICATIONS DATA
Siksikaitsitapi: Stories of the Blackfoot People

Many Guns, Payne; Many Fingers, Crystal; Potts, Sheena; Calf Robe Latasha;
Fox, Tim; Yellow Horn Marlene; Starlight, DerRic.
Foreword: Many Guns, Alayna

1. Indigenous Language | 2. First Nations | 3. Truth and Reconciliation

These stories were originally published in The Calgary Public Library's Treaty 7 Language Series.
Reprinted with permission by The Calgary Public Library. Special thanks to Rosemary Griebel.

The mentors and publishers of this series have supported the authors to share their stories
under the guidance of traditional language speakers and Elders including
Shirlee Crow Shoe, Colleen Sitting Eagle, and Sheena Potts

Durvile & UpRoute Books Spirit of Nature Series.
Series editor, Raymond Yakeleya

978-1-988824-83-3 (pbk) | 978-1-988824-88-8 (e-book)
978-1-988824-89-5 (audiobook)

Front cover illustration, Payne Many Guns. Jacket and book design, Lorene Shyba.
Thanks to Susan Kristoferson for paste paper texture and Jennifer Theroux for copy editing, English.

Durvile Publications would like to acknowledge the financial support of the Government of Canada through
the Canadian Heritage Canada Book Fund and the Government of Alberta, Alberta Media Fund.

First edition, first printing. 2022. Printed in China.

Durvile honours the traditional land upon which our studios rest. The Indigenous Peoples of Southern Alberta
include the Siksika, Piikani, and Kainai of the Blackfoot Confederacy; the Dene Tsuut'ina;
the Chiniki, Bearspaw, and Wesley Stoney Nakoda First Nations; and the Region 3 Métis Nation of Alberta.

DEDICATION

We dedicate this book
to the memory of our children
who didn't make it home from
Indian Residential School.

In your thoughts, prayers, and actions,
please continue to
stand beside us in our goals
of reconciliation.

CONTENTS

• • • •

CONTENTS

• • • •

Oki Iitahmikskanotoni

*Hello, It is a
Good Day
Today*

. . . .

Oki Iitahmikskanotoni

*Hello, It is a
Good Day Today*

PHOTO: LORENE SHYBA

Alayna Many Guns
Sohkapinaaki

I AM THRILLED to welcome you all to this beautiful Blackfoot cultural experience. These children's book chapters are written, illustrated, and translated by various Blackfoot Elders, authors, and artists to share, firsthand, a snapshot of our strong, beautiful way of life.

Siksikaitsitapi is a Blackfoot word that means "all things Blackfoot." This includes people, our traditional lands, the way we do things, and our customs. It is a powerful word in our culture identifying our existence. Today, Siksikaitsitapi also encompasses our modern-day Tribal Nations of the Siksika Nation, the Blood Tribe, the Piikani Nation, and the Blackfeet Tribe which together make up the Blackfoot Confederacy. Our traditional lands since time immemorial encompass the southern Canadian provinces of Alberta and Saskatchewan and into the northern half of the present-day US State of Montana. Although we are all Niitsitapi, minimal differences are present in the way each Tribe speaks, writes and interprets our language.

As Niitsitapi, Blackfoot People, our language, culture and stories are the foundation of our existence. Stories are sacred and are used as educational tools for not only our younger generations, but for all our people when we consult with Elders and our Grandfathers and Grandmothers. Stories include paradigms by our Elders to educate about the ways our ancestors did things, and also about ways our ancestors did *not* do things

One of my most treasured stories includes Natoosi, the Sun. A Grandfather shared his remembrance of waking early as a child as the sun was rising over the land. He heard his father sacredly drumming and singing to welcome Natoosi humbly, asking for prayers for the People, giving thanks for our many gifts and honouring our existence. As Niitsitapi we continue to practice our traditional ceremonies as given to us by Natoosi, Creator, and our Holy Ones. We hold in high esteem the sacredness of our cultural practices and acknowledge that our most sacred ways are not be to written down nor shared freely. Strict protocol is implemented to protect and ensure that the traditional methods of teaching and learning are continued.

These Blackfoot children's book chapters share common knowledge stories which have been shared to our authors. Common knowledge includes everyday lessons and norms. The book provides us with an opportunity to reclaim our truths. In the past, sitting with an Elder and listening to traditional stories of the stars, the animals, Napi, and our purpose was a great gift. Today, this is more important than ever. Elders gift us with purpose, strength, knowledge, and love.

Throughout the last century and a half, in spite of Indian Residential Schools, colonized legislation, and laws created to 'erase in the Indian in the child,' the Niitsitapi have persevered in carrying on our stories. Niitsitapi have always cherished and valued the sacredness of the child. Children are considered holy and are held in high esteem. The loss of our children in the time of Residential Schools and being in a childless society was devastating. I ask that you keep our children who never made it home from Indian Residential School in your thoughts and prayers, and that you continue to stand beside us in our goals of reconciliation.

I invite you to experience this book, *Siksikaitsitapi: Stories of the Blackfoot People* to share a glimpse of our captivating Blackfoot way of life. *Siksikaitsitapi* will be a wonderful resource for many. I thank the numerous people that have supported us in the creation of these books, especially Richard Van Camp and the people at the Calgary Public Library, and Lorene Shyba and Raymond Yakeleya of Durvile & UpRoute Books.

— *Sohkapinaaki, Alayna Many Guns, 2022*
Member of the Siksika Nation

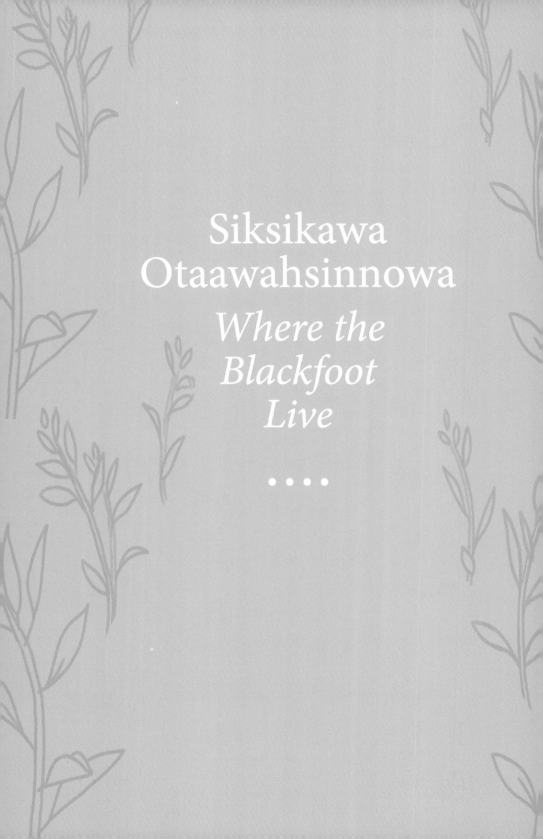

Siksikawa Otaawahsinnowa

Where the Blackfoot Live

....

A STORY BY PAYNE MANY GUNS

Siksikawa Otaawahsinnowa

Where the Blackfoot Live

Payne Many Guns
Iikootsomin (*Red Wing*)

Illustrated by Payne Many Guns

Dedication

Oki nohkoo'sah Siksikawa

Siksikaitsitapi Okosoowaiks

To the Children

of the Blackfoot Confederacy.

— *Payne Many Guns*

Siksika itopiya sokiohs

Blackfoot People live on the plains.

● ● ● ●

Siksika itopiya spahko

Blackfoot People live on the hills.

Kaiyskahpaiks — *Porcupine Hills*

Omahsatsiko — *Great Sandhills*

Katoyiiskiks — *Sweetgrass Hills*

● ● ● ●

Siksika itopiya miistakkiitsi

Blackfoot People live in the mountains.

Ninastako — *Chief Mountain*

Miista'ksskowa — *Castle Mountain*

Omahkaisto — *Crowsnest Mountain*

● ● ● ●

Siksika itopiya nitahtaan

Blackfoot People live along the rivers.

Mohkin'stitahtaan — *Bow River*

Otahkaitaam — *Yellowstone River*

Ponokaisitahtaan — *North Saskatchewan River*

● ● ● ●

Siksika ohpokopiya sooyiipiiksiiksi

Blackfoot People live with the water animals.

Mamii — *Fish*

Amonisii — *Otter*

Ksistakii — *Beaver*

• • • •

13

Siksika ohpokopiya kanomiyanitsipiiksiiks

Blackfoot People live with the land animals.

Iinii — *Bison*

Ponoka — *Elk*

Miisinsskii — *Badger*

● ● ● ●

Siksika ohpokopiya miistakkiitsi ootsipisattsi piiksiiks

Blackfoot People live with the mountain animals.

Paksikoyi — *Bear*

Naataayo — *Lynx*

Mistaksaomahkihkina — *Mountain Goat*

• • • •

15

Siksika ohpokopiya spommiipiiksiiks

Blackfoot People live with the sky animals.

Piiksii — *Bird*

Maisto — *Crow*

Piita — *Eagle*

• • • •

Siksika ohpokopiya iskssiinaiks

Blackfoot People live with the insects.

Naamoo — *Bee*

Kwowawakaasi — *Spider*

Aisko'kiinam — *Ant*

● ● ● ●

Siksika itaisspoipiya piisaatsaiskiitsi kii sa'amiitsi

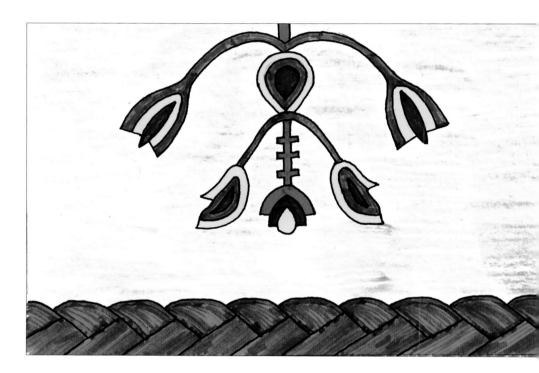

Blackfoot People live with the plants and medicine.

Siipatsimaan — *Sweetgrass*

Okonoki — *Saskatoon Berry*

Kakitsimo — *Mint*

● ● ● ●

Siksika itaisspoipiya piisaatsaiskiitsi kii sa'amiitsi

Blackfoot People live in the cities.

Mohkinstsis — *Calgary*

Omahkoyis — *Edmonton*

Sikoohkotok — *Lethbridge*

● ● ● ●

Siksika itopiya
annistsi ihkootspitsi ksahko

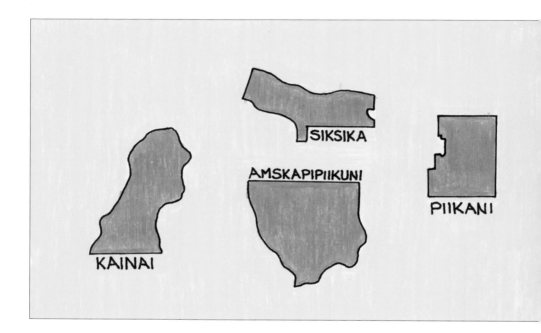

Blackfoot People live on reserves.

Siksika
Kainai
Piikani
Amskapi Piikuni

• • • •

Siksika itaistahtopi kakatoosiiks

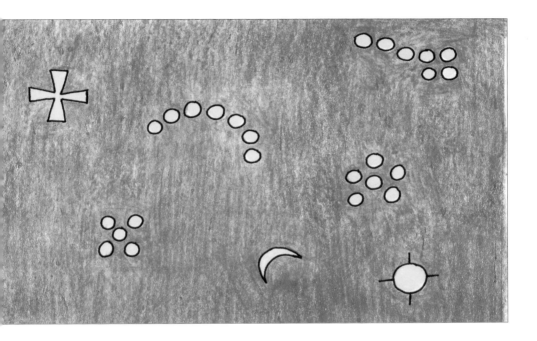

Most importantly, Blackfoot People live under the stars.

Iipisoowaahs — *Morning Star*

Ihkitsikammiksi — *Big Dipper*

Mioohpoiksi — *Bunched Stars*

● ● ● ●

Kitaisskiinipa otsitopihpi Siksikawa

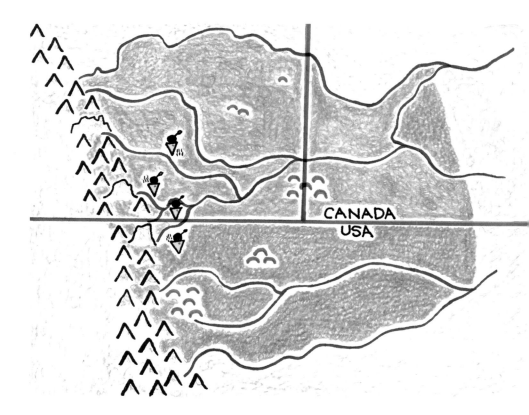

Now you know where the Blackfoot People live.

————— *Kyaan* —————

About the Author

Payne Many Guns

My name is Payne Many Guns. My traditional name is Iikootsomin which means *"Red Wing."* It is my great-great-grandfather's name that I am honoured to have. I am a member of the Siksika Nation which is part of the Blackfoot Confederacy. I come from a long line of chiefs and signatories of Treaty 7. I am also the founder and owner of Niitsitapi Co. which is an Indigenous clothing brand. I am very passionate about my language and culture because of the knowledge, pride, strength, and resiliency it gives me.

Acknowledgements

I would like to acknowledge my mom, Alayna Many Guns, and our Blackfoot Elders. I would also like to acknowledge Mookakoyis (Calgary Public Library) and Durvile & UpRoute Books for identifying reconciliation as a priority, and their continued support of Indigenous People. My artwork is inspired by my Blackfoot culture and our stories, which all relate to our way of life. I appreciate everyone who has contributed to this amazing and brilliant project. Lastly, and most importantly, I would like to acknowledge the Creator who has given us the strength to continue the journey of reconciliation.

A'pistotooki kii Ihkitsik Kaawa'pomaahkaa

Creator and the Seven Animals

• • • •

A'pistotooki kii Ihkitsik Kaawa'pomaahkaa

Creator and the Seven Animals

Crystal Many Fingers

Illustrated by Alex Soop

Dedication

I wish to begin by dedicating this work to my daughter,
Patricia Elena Soop and
my son, Alexander Shawn Soop.
These two young people have been with me since
I became a young mom.
Our little tri-pod has given me much
love, laughter, and joy in my life.
Also, to Part B of my family, Dixie, Tony, and Dr. Mo.
Thanks for growing up with me and for looking after me
through the difficult times in our childhood.
To Barry, without you I could never have accomplished
the things that I have done.
And lastly, Mom and Dad
(Dr. Helen and Wallace Manyfingers),
I know that your spirits watch over us and we all miss
and love you very much!

—*Crystal Many Fingers*

It was **iksisto** (hot) on a **niipo** (summer) morning, **Natosi** (the sun) was shining brightly in the **sspoohtsi** (sky).

Seven of the **kaawa'pomaahkaa** (animals) had gathered together to say their regular morning **aatsimoyihkaan** (prayers).

They were seated in an **ao'takii** (a circle).

"Ayo Ihtsipaitapiiyao'p
(O Great Spirit and Source of Life)

Ayo A'pistotooki *(Our Creator)*

Isspommookinnaan *(Help us)*"

Immoyiitapi *(Bigfoot)* led the group as they asked
A'pistotooki *(Creator)* for help from harm.

After they said **Aatssimoyihkaan** (prayers),
Ksisskstaki (Beaver), the one who had
sopoksistawa'si (grown in wisdom) asked,
*"Why did **A'pistotooki** (Creator) put us here on this
Ksaahkomm (Earth)?"*
All of the other **kaawa'pomaahkaa** (animals)
nodded their heads in agreement.
*"Yes, please O Great Spirit, **A'pistotooki,** tell us why
we were put here on this **Ksaahkomm** (Earth)."*

29

All of a sudden, **waahkanaapinako** *(a beautiful sunbeam)*

shone down through the **soksistsiko** *(clouds)*.

It shone directly down on the **kaawa'pomaahkaa** *(animals)*.

All of them looked up **sspoohtsi** *(skyward)*.

A loud voice began to speak,

"I am **A'pistotooki** *(your Creator)*.

I will now tell you why you have each been put on this **Ksaahkomm** *(Earth)*."

"**Ksisskstaki** *(Beaver),* since you are the first one to ask and since you cherish the knowledge, you will be the one to **Sopoksistawa'si** *(grow in wisdom).*

You will have the gift of being able to move the **Aohkii** *(water)* and you will protect it and all who dwells in them.

You will also protect the **maohtoksko** *(trees)* and **soi'stipikiaaki** *(berries)* that also live along the **niitahtaa** *(river).*

This will greatly help the **Niitsitapi** *(Real People).*

The **Niitsitapi** will always honour the great **Aohkii iksissta'pssi** *(water spirits)* in their **Aatssimoyihkaan** *(prayers)*."

"**Kiaayo** *(Bear),* you are the protector
of the **ikso'kowa** *(relatives),*
the **Nookoossinnaaniksi** *(children),*
Ninnaaniksi *(fathers),*
Niksisstsinnanniksi *(mothers),* and
Naahsinnanniksi *(Grandparents)*
of the **Niitsitapi** *(Real People).*

Because of this, you will always be
sskonata'pssi *(industrious and strong).*

You will be **iiyikitapiiyi** *(brave and fearless)*
as you roam the **Ksaahkomm** *(Earth).*

You will be considered an
awaawahkao'tsii *(warrior)* to all
because of how you strive to protect them."

"**Piita** *(Eagle),* your gift is the gift of **akomimm** *(love).*

Because of you, my **ksaahkomm** *(Earth)* will be **ikkinaa'pssi** *(gentle and peaceful).*

You will bring **ikkinaa'pssi** *(peace)* to the world as you **soy'sksissi** *(fly high in the sky).*

The **Niitsitapi** will thank you for this as they cherish your **sooa'tsis** *(tail feathers).*

They will **iiyikihkaohsit** *(dance)* in your honour."

"**Innii** *(Buffalo)*, your gift from me is the gift of **iniiyimm** *(respect)* and **Sstsaakat** *(admiration and praise)*.

Your kind will provide all of the **aoowahsin** *(food)* and your hides will give the **Niitsitapi okooyi** *(shelter)* to help them survive.

The **Niitsitapi** shall **akomimm** *(love)* you until the end of time."

"**Makoyi,** *(Wolf)*, you will show the
Niitsitapi not to act **o'tsitska'pssi** *(selfish)*.

You will teach them that they are
naato *(sacred)* to **Niisto** *(me)*.

The **Niitsitapi** will look up to you
beside the **Iipisowaahs** *(Morning Star)*
when they feel **Oyiitsi'taki** *(sad and mournful)*.

"**Sspopii** (Turtle), your beautiful shell
will be a record of what I have told you all today.

You will keep this knowledge for all of time
for the **Niitsitapi.**

They will know that what I say is the
omanissin (truth)."

"And last but not least, **Immoyiitapi** *(Bigfoot)*.

Kiisto *(You)* will not be seen by everyone but they will know that you **itstsii** *(exist)*.

Because of this, you will walk **okamo't** *(straight, honest and upright)*.

This is why you will be **spii** (tall) like the **Mo'toisspitaiksi** *(All Tall People Clan)*."

After **A'pistotooki** was finished speaking, each **kaawa'pomaahkaa** went their separate ways.

They knew now why they were put here.

They are here to help the **Niitsitapi**.

As they left, other **kaawa'pomaahkaa** could be seen waiting in line to ask **A'pistotooki** for the reason why they were here as well.

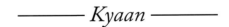

——— *Kyaan* ———

About the Author

Crystal Many Fingers

Crystal is a Blackfoot member of the Kainai First Nation of Treaty 7. She grew up on the Blood Reserve and as a child roamed the halls of the University of Lethbridge where her mother, Dr. Helen Manyfingers, was studying to earn her Bachelor of Education degree. This inspired Crystal to enroll at the University of Calgary, where she chose to major in English Literature. After completing her B.A., Crystal decided to pursue a career in teaching, to follow in the footsteps of three of her siblings. She then went on to complete her Master of Education degree with a specialty in Adult and Workplace Environmental Learning. She now works as the Indigenous Consultant to Curriculum at Bow Valley College in Calgary, Alberta.

Aakomimmihtanii
Love

. . . .

Aakomimmihtanii
Love

Sheena Potts

Mai'stoistowaakii *(Crow Pretty Woman)*

Illustrated by Kristy North Peigan

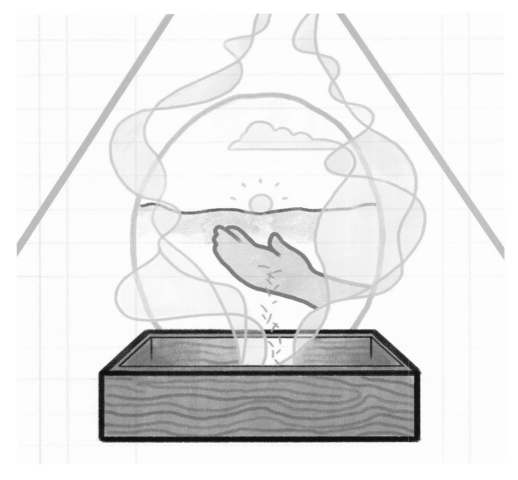

Aakomimmihtaanii iitomatapa'piiwa aisopoyinakosi
Love is the first ray of the morning sun.

Kii aamatoo'pi aamoto'simaani
And the smell of sweetpine smudge.

Aakomimmmihtaani iinakowa ama I'naksipoka asistsiksskiaakis
Love is the bright smile on Baby's face.

Iitatsiiyihka'sa
And the room lights up with pride.

Aakomimmihtaani aaksomo'toosi ani kiiksisstonoon osinao'sskiposin

Love is the feel of Mama's soft lips kissing chubby cheeks.

Kii Kinnoona otato'tookasini.

And the security of Daddy's strong hug.

Aakomimmihtaani anni
kitakasinipoka imitawa
Love is the slobbery lick from the doggy's tongue.

Kii I'taamaawatoyaapikssi
And tail happily wagging to greet the day.

Aakomimmihtaani anni issapinosini
Love is the wiping away of tears.

Kii itayikitapiiyi'op
And learning to face fear.

Aakomimmihtaani anni
Kaaahsi awaatsimoyihkaa'si
Love is the tender voice of Grandmother's prayers.

Kii Kaaahsi aawatoyanihkssi
And the drum beat of the
Grandfather's ceremony song.

Aakomimmihtaani anni ksisstsokomm attsistohkomisi

Love is the first sound of thunder when spring comes.

Aakomimmihtaani anni iiyoohtsipi sootaayi otsiksiitstomi ksaahkomm

Love is the sound of raindrops nourishing the earth.

Kii iitomatapissi maan paitapisini

And new life begins.

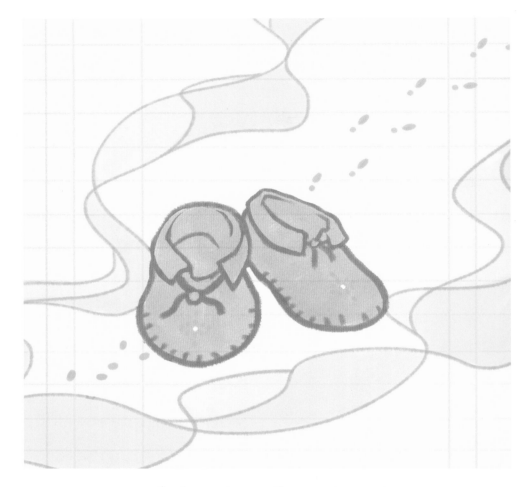

Aakomimmihtaani anni maatomiksikkayit kitaapo'toko.
Love is those first steps that set you free.

Aakomimmihtaani anni a'pistotsipi niipaitapiiyssini ksikka'sini
Love is the life that builds you step by step.

Kii ksikka'sini, sataamisini kii satammisini
And, breath by breath.

Kii kiitomatomatapo aakomimmihtaani.
*And knowing your journey
began with love.*

—— *Kyaan* ——

Aatsimmoiyihkanni
Spirituality

Kimmapiiypitsinni
Kindness to others

Innakotsiiysinni
Respect for others

Ihpipototsp
Purpose for being there

Nitsisitapiiysinni
To be Blackfoot

Akisistoypaittapiisinni
Being able to take on tasks independently

Isspomaanitapiiysinni
To be helpful

Aoahkannaistokawa
Everything comes in pairs (balance)

Ihnkanaitapstiwa
Everything is provided to do what you want.

Pommotsiiysinni
To transfer something to others (knowledge)

Kakyosin
Be aware of your environment

About the Author

Sheena Potts

Mai'stoistowaakii *(Crow Pretty Woman)*

Niitsi Piikaniaakii

I am a Piikani lady/woman.

Nitsikohtatsiika'si nokosiksi kii nisotana

I am a proud mother and grandmother.

Niitsikoyikitomai'takapinaan Siksitaitapisini

We practise the ways of Siksikasitapi.

Niitsininamsskaapinaan

We belong to the Thunder Pipe Society.

Iyipposstoyiitsi nitaanist ksinima'tstohoki'p

I have been an educator for thirty years.

Dedication

To my son Siipisaahkomaapi.

May you always remember

how much you are loved.

And to all little boys with braids:

You are strong,

You are resilient,

and most importantly

You are loved by so many.

— *Latasha Calf Robe*

Niitsippooktsistaanitsi

My Braids

Latasha Calf Robe

Matoomiikamoosaaki

(First Steals Woman)

Oki, Niisto anakok Siipisaahkomaapi

Hello, I am 'Night Boy.'

● ● ● ●

Niitsippooktsistaanitsi, Latasha Calf Robe

Niiokska nitsiipootsiitstanistsi

I have three braids.

● ● ● ●

Na'ah nitiyamstinnomook kanaksistsiikoos

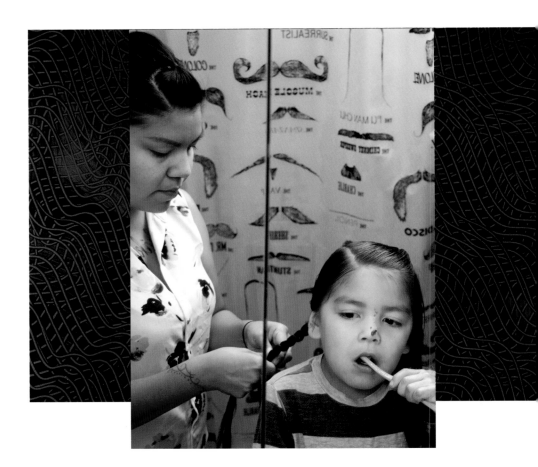

My mom braids my hair every day.

● ● ● ●

Niitsippooktsistaanitsi, Latasha Calf Robe

Na'ah nitiyamstinnomook tska niitsiikakomimmook

My mom braids my hair because she loves me.

● ● ● ●

Ninnaa nitaawaistamatsook nitahkaniistatoitsiikaatopiiya niitsippooktsistaanitsi

My dad shows me how to take care of my braids.

● ● ● ●

Ninnaa iikastonnatohtsiitsiiskaasi Niitsippooktsistaanitsi

*My dad is so proud
of my braids.*

● ● ● ●

Naaáhsiksi awaanii niitsiikohtsookaas niitsippooktsistaanitsi

*My grandparents say
my braids make me strong.*

● ● ● ●

Naaáhsiksi awaanii Niitsiikhtowaakomimookoh Niitsippooktsistaanitsi

My grandparents say
my braids bring me love.

● ● ● ●

Nitawwootahkatoop niitsippooktsistaanitsi

My braids keep me safe.

● ● ● ●

Niitsikohtsookhsipatapi niitsippooktsistaanitsi

My braids keep me healthy.

• • • •

Nitsikakomitsiip
Nistippooktsistaanitsi

I love my braids.

——— *Kyaan* ———

Blackfoot Kinship

Níkso'kowaiksa — *My Family*

Niisto — *Me*

Na'ah — *Mom*

Ninna — *Dad*

Naaáhsiksi — *Grandparents*

Nii'saa — *Older brother*

Ninsstaa — *Older sister*

Issitsíimaan — *Baby*

About the Author

Latasha Calf Robe

Matoomiikamoosaaki *(First Steals Woman)*

Oki, niisto annista Matoomiikamoosaaki.

Ninna anni-sta Onistaahsiinaam.

Niiksissta annista Sahksiisinaki.

Naahsaa annista Naapiiaakii, Jija Ts'ika,
Pîmōpakihō, Steven Calf Robe.

First Steals Woman (Latasha Calf Robe) is from the Kainaiwa First Nation, otherwise known as the Blood Tribe. Latasha is the proud daughter of Marvin and Teena Calf Robe. Her grandparents are Carolla Calf Robe, Shirley Starlight, Steven Calf Robe, and William Auger. Latasha is a mother of three beautiful Blackfoot children whom she raises with her partner, Adam Solway. With the support and teachings from her family, Latasha is thrilled to share Niitsippooktsistaanitsi with you.

Photos throughout the story: Athina Sofocleous
Brokenhead Ojiway Nation

Napi kii Imitaa

Napi and the Dogs

....

Napi kii Imitaa
Napi and the Dogs

Tim Fox
Natoyi'sokasiim

*Illustrations: Keegan Starlight and
Amanda Fox-Starlight*

Dedication

I grew up on the Blood Reserve, raised with teachings of my family lineage, Kainai (gah-nah) culture, history and values. I continue to learn our ways until this day and for days to come.

My mother, Connie Fox (Mills), was once an interpreter for the Head-Smashed-In Buffalo Jump, a UNESCO World Heritage site. One of my fondest childhood memories was of my mother sharing creation stories, or Napi (nah-be) stories, as we refer to them. I remember her telling me these stories in detail and then, together, we would talk about the story and identify the lessons/teachings from each story. These lessons, this memory, and those times together with my mother have helped to shape the person I am today and the parent I am today.

For this, I dedicate this book to my mother. Thank you for this important life lesson. Hand to heart for you and these teachings.

— *Your son, Tim*

Prologue

Characters in this story are:
Napi/Crow, Dog, Mice, Thunder, Rain, and Bison Skull.

There is diversity within our Indigenous nations across Mother Earth. Depending on where you come from, there are many variations and teachings of each community, Tribe, Nation, Peoples' values, customs, beliefs, protocol, history, and Creation.

This story is one of those teachings from a **Kainai** perspective of a trickster character we know as **Napi**.

My mother shared this story with me as a child and is a story I think about often. I was inspired by the lessons of this story and are ones that I now teach my daughter, Charm **Naataawaybyo-akii** (Nah-da-way-byo-ah-gee).

Napi is a significant being, character and trickster within Blackfoot culture. There are very sacred **Napi** stories that I do not know, or even if I did know them, I would not have the permission to share so publicly. This story is not one of those sacred stories but a story of "Why things are the way they are." I hope you enjoy and please be sure to have a discussion after reading about the lessons from this story.

In **Siksikaitsitapi** (sik-sik-ate-sit-ah-bee), Blackfoot Confederacy teachings, **Napi** is a character with the ability to shape into any form, animate or inanimate.

On this particular day,
Napi was flying high in the sky as
issapo (is-saa-bo), crow.

As **issapo** was enjoying the beauty of **Siksikaitsitapi** territory, he came across **Imitaa (ee-mee-daa),** dog.

Napi swooped down to **Imitaa** and asked,
"Oki (oh-gee), tsaa niitapii (tsa-knee-da-be)?

Hello, how are you?" **Imitaa** answered,

"Oki Napi, sukapii (sue-ga-be)! Hello, **Napi**, I'm good."

Napi said, **"Tsima (tsima)?**
Da-ga kiisto (dah-gah-gee-stoo) Where are you going?

Imitaa said, "I'm just enjoying this beautiful land
on this day gifted to us by
Apistotokii (ah-bis-da-doe-gee), Creator."

As they were wandering
sawkiosti (saw-gee-oat-see), the prairies,
they heard the sounds of celebration in
the distance and decided to follow the sounds to
see what was happening.
They came upon an abandoned **inii (ee-knee),**
buffalo skull.

From inside came the sounds of
laughter and celebration.
Oki, taka kisto (da-ga-gee-stoo)
Hello, who's there?
Akaipii (ah-gay-bee)
What's going on?

Just then **kaanaiskiinaa (gaa-ness-gee-naa),**
mouse, poked its head out of the abandoned **inii** skull
and greeted **Napi kii Imitaa.**
"Oki, we are just having a celebration
and **ahtsisaki (aht-see-sah-gee)** feast."

Imitaa said, "Sounds like you're all having
an amazing celebration. Can we join you?"

Kaanaiskiinaa said,

"**Aa** (ah) yes, **kiisto (gee-stoo)** you can

join our celebration but there are

a couple of rules to follow before you can join.

First, you must be respectful to everyone inside.

Next, you must show our **natoyis (nah-doy-is)**

home respect and not make a mess.

Finally, one of the most important instructions,

you must remove your tail to shrink down

to a size small enough to enter our **natoyis.**

Then **kiisto** can join in our celebration and feast."

So **Imitaa** followed all the rules
and they had a full afternoon of
laughter, visits, celebration,
and feasting!

Imitaa had such a wonderful time
at the celebration that the next day
he returned with more **Imitaa** to ask if they
can all join in the celebrations.

Again, **Kaanaiskiinaa** reminded
them all of the rules:
"**Kiisto** must be respectful to everyone inside.
Kiisto must show our home respect and
not make a mess. One of the
most important instructions is **kiisto**
must remove your tail to shrink down
to a size small enough to enter our home, and,
when **kiisto** leave, it is very, very, very important
that **kiisto** leave with your own tail.
If you follow all these rules and instructions,
then you can join in our celebration and feast."

All the **Imitaa** agreed and one by one,
they removed their tail at the entrance,
shrunk to the size of **Kaanaiskiinaa** and
entered the celebration.
Again, they had an afternoon full of
laughter, visits and feasting.
They were having so much fun that they
lost track of the time and
as night fell,
they heard the sound of
ksistikoom (git-sis-dee-goom)
thunder and **sootah (sue-dah)** rain.

In a mad scramble to get **natoyis**

and not be caught in the **sootah**,

they forgot about all the rules

given to them by **Kaanaiskiinaa**.

They began to scream and
trip over one another

in a rush to the entrance to

grab their tail and run **natoyis**.

They were tripping over each other,

making a mess and grabbing

any tail as they made an exit into the **sootah**.

And so, there are many lessons
we can learn from this story.

Imitaa will never forget one of these lessons to this day

because what is one thing you see **Imitaa** doing to

other **Imitaa** when they meet each other?

They're looking for their own tails!

——— *The End* ———

About the Author

Tim Fox, Natoyi'sokasiim

Tim Fox is a proud member of the Kainai, Blood Tribe, within Siksikaitsitapi, Blackfoot Confederacy. His family comes from the Ahkaipohkaaks (Many Children's) Clan. His parents are Mike and Connie Fox (Mills) and late Grandparents, Emma (George) Many Feathers, Stephen Fox Sr., Virginia Mills and Jim Chief Calf. Tim currently lives and works in Mohkinstis (Calgary). He is the Vice President of Indigenous Relations for the Calgary Foundation. He is blessed and grateful to be helping raise his beautiful daughter, Charm, along with her mom, Dawn Fox (Sanders).

Acknowledgements

This project would not be possible if it weren't, first and foremost, for the Blackfoot People and ways. I often think that we are not the fastest growing segment of the population by coincidence, but we are the answered prayers of our ancestors, who prayed for the survival of our people and our ways! I thank Creator each and every day for all my blessings and my challenges. Thank you to the Calgary Public Library and Durvile & UpRoute Books. Our future generations are in good hands with people like you making significant strides toward a better future for all! I thank my family and friends who've helped to shape the person I am today. Hand to heart to all of you!

Omahkitapiksi Okakinikiiwa

Teachings from our Elders

· · · ·

Omahkitapiksi Okakinikiiwa

Teachings from our Elders

Marlene Yellow Horn
Iikiinayookaa

Illustrated by Smith Wright

Dedication

Saapaata, Iikiinayookaa, and I'tsaapoyi

This book is dedicated to
Saapaata Wacey Coleman Rabbit
and to my grandchildren not yet born.

May you always take time to learn from
our Elders and continue our
Siksikaitsitapi ways.
Hand to heart in gratitude for
choosing me to be your Na'ah.

— *Marlene Yellow Horn*

Do you know how powerful Siksikaitsitapi people are?

Kitsskinii'pa *Do you know* **maanstataato'sipi** *how powerful* **Siksikatsitapiwa** *Blackfoot People*

Our Elders knew that World War I ended long before anyone else did.

They could see the soldiers marching home in the clouds.

Omahkitapiksi *Elders/old people*

iiyaksskinima *knew already*

otakssikaaa wahkaootsisawa *end of the war,*

matoom awahkaootsini *World War I.*

Ipapainoyiwa *like a dream scene*

soowaksi *soldiers*

aahkiaapiwaakayiwa *marching home*

amotsi soksistsikoistsi *in the clouds.*

*Our Elders teach us when we feel
unbalanced or disconnected
we need to return to the land.
The land will remind us who we are
as Blackfoot People,
the original people of this land.*

Omahkitapiksi *Elders*

ai'stamattsokiwa *teach us*

sawasokimmohsopi
not feeling good

kitasskitapoot kitawahsiim
return your land.

Niinastako *(Chief Mountain)*

103

*Our Elders teach the importance
of having a pet dog.*

Omahkitapiksi *Elders*
ai'stamattsokiwa *teach us*
iiko'totamapiwa *important*
Oaaksskani'taamsosi iimitaa
pet dog.

(Left to Right) Patsy Rabbit, Doris Many Guns (back right),
Beatrice Goodstriker, Frank Goodstriker (sitting in middle).

Dogs provide companionship,
and physical and spiritual safety.

Iimitaiksi
dogs

iikasokohpokaopiimayiwa
we live with them well.

Our Elders teach us to always call our spirit
with us by saying, "Let's go."
We want to keep our physical body and spirit
together to ensure balance.

Omahkitapiksi *Elders*

ai'stamattsokiwa *teach us*

inihkatsimatsiiwa kottaka
call your spirit

awaanopa *say* **"Okiah"** *Let's go.*

Iitasokimmohsopa *feel good.*

*Our Elders teach us that
everything happens in its time.*

Omahkitapiksi
Elders

ai'stamattsokiwa
teach us

I'tsini oohkia'piitsiki
everything happens.

Larry Rabbit and Katie Rabbit.

My child, it is important to always take time to visit and learn from our Elders.

Iiko'totaamapiwa *It is important*

aakoksisawaatsi *to always visit*

Omahkitapiksi *Elders*

——— *The End* ———

About the Author
Marlene Yellow Horn

Iikiinayookaa Marlene Yellow Horn is a Blackfoot author and educator from the Mamoyiksi Fish Eater Clan of the Kainai First Nation. She is a mother to Saapaata Wacey Rabbit, professional hockey player, has been married for thirty years to I'tsaapoyi Marvin Yellow Horn, and is the only daughter of the late Larry and Patsy Rabbit. Iikiinayookaa received her Master of Education (2010), Bachelor of Education (2005), and Bachelor of Management (1998) from the University of Lethbridge. She is the current Principal at Piitoayis Family School, Calgary Board of Education.

Iikiinayookaa grew up in the community of Old Agency, Kainai First Nation. She spent many summers rodeoing with her family; connecting her to the spirit of the ponokaomitaa horse and the love of all animals. She loved to spend time with her grandparents, Rita and Bill Rabbit and Frank and Beatrice Goodstriker, who taught her the traditional protocols of the Siksikaitsitapi Blackfoot people. She has fond memories of her great grandmother, Katie Rabbit, sharing stories in the old Blackfoot dialect. Her childhood was filled with laughter, stories, and sport. She participates in Niinaamskaan Thunder/Medicine Pipe Bundle ceremonies in the spring, sacred tobacco ceremonies in the winter, and draws strength from the annual Aakookaatsin Sundance held in the summer at the sacred hills of the Belly Buttes. She is tasked as the harvester of sage and sweetgrass for her family. She takes pride in knowing her sage has travelled the world, providing protection and prayer for her son. She currently makes her home in Mohkinitsi Calgary, Alberta.

Ipisoowatsis Nomohpapiiyihpiksi

Morning Star's Family

....

Ipisoowatsis Nomohpapiiyihpiksi
Morning Star's Family

DerRic Starlight
Illustrated by DerRic Starlight

Dedication

This story is dedicated to
daughter Jessica Snyder-Starlight.

Special thanks to:
mother Carol Mason, father Jesse Starlight,
the Calgary Public Library, and
Durvile & UpRoute Books.

— DerRic Starlight

Oki nisto nitanikoo Ipisoowatsis

Hello my name is Morning Star.

I am seven **(ihkitsik)** years old.

I like to draw
on the computer with Paint.

This is my story.

I am happy you are here.

Niiksissta Napiyaki
My mother is White.

Ninna is Nitstitapi
My father is Native/First Nations.

We live in the city of Calgary **(Mohkintsis)**.

I have three **(niooksa)** sets
of Grandparents **(naahsiiks)**.

Ni'tokskaa, Naato'k, Niookska
One, Two, Three.

Don't be confused.
I will explain.

Naahsiiks are napikwaans
My first Grandparents are White

Naahsiiks are nitstitapi
My second Grandparents are First Nations.

Naahsiiks are napikwaan kii nitstita-pi
My third Grandparents are White and First Nations.

When my dad was young,
his mother and father separated and married
my other Grandparents. Don't be worried.
They are all friends **(itakkaa).**
They are happy people and
respect **(iinakotsiiynii)** one another.

I like to dance at the pow-wow.

My Native Grandma **(Na'ahks)** and
White Grandpa **(Na'ahks)** make my outfit.

My White Grandpa **(Na'ahks)** and
Native Grandma **(Na'ahks)** drive me to the
pow-wow in their car.

My Native Grandparents
love watching me dance
at the pow-wow.

I am happy to make my
mother **(niiksissta)** and
father **(niina)** proud **(iyihka'si)**.

There are different families from all over
the world **(ksaahko)**
who come to watch me dance.

I dance for my
First Nations (**Nitsitapiiminaaniksi**)
and White People (**Napiikwaaks**).

At the pow-wow all my family dance together
in a great big round dance
(O'taksipasskaan).

This makes the Creator **(Apistotooki)** proud
of all families who dance together.

I am proud **(itsiiyihka'si)** of who I am!

Being proud of who you are
makes you strong **(sskonata'pssi).**

—— *Kyaan* ——

About the Author/Illustrator
DerRic Starlight

DerRic Starlight is from the Tsuut'ina Nation west of Calgary, Alberta, and can also trace his ancestry to the Blackfoot Confederacy. He is a comedian, puppeteer, screenwriter, and pro-wrestling promoter. At a young age DerRic wanted to become a creative writer and producer of puppets for television like his idol, Jim Henson. At the age of 17, he set out to follow his dream studying at film and acting schools in Vancouver, Toronto, and Scottsdale, Arizona. DerRic has created his own cast of Native puppet characters and has travelled all over North America since 1997. He has starred in many different television productions with The Aboriginal Peoples Television Network (APTN) and has won the prestigious Gemini Award of Canada as a voice actor. In 2021 DerRic became an official puppeteer with The Jim Henson Company.

Durvile.com

Books in the UpRoute Spirit of Nature Series

Series Editors: Raymond Yakeleya and Lorene Shyba

The Tree by the Woodpile and Other Dene Spirit of Nature Tales
Raymond Yakeleya
Illustrations: Deborah Desmarais

978-1-988824-03-1 *(pbk)* | 978-1-988824-52-9 *(audiobook)*
978-1-988824-16-1 *(e-book)*

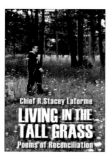

Living in the Tall Grass: Poems of Reconciliation
Chief R. Stacey Laforme

978-1-988824-05-5 *(pbk)* | 978-1-988824-32-1 *(audiobook)*
978-0-968975-49-7 *(e-book)*

Lillian & Kokomis: The Spirit of Dance
Lynda Partridge
Foreword: Chief R. Stacey Laforme
Illustrations: Dave Nicholson
Winner of the Alberta Publishers Children & Y/A Award 2020
978-1-988824-27-7 *(pbk)* | 978-1-988824-29-1 *(audiobook)*
978-1-988824-28-4 *(e-book)*

We Remember the Coming of the White Man, First Edition
Authors: Elizabeth Yakeleya, Sarah Simon *et al*
Editor: Sarah Stewart
Foreword: Raymond Yakeleya

978-1-988824-24-6 *(pbk)* | 978-1-988824-37-6 *(audiobook)*
978-1-988824-56-7 *(e-book)*

Books in the UpRoute Spirit of Nature Series

We Remember the Coming of the White Man, Special Edition
Authors: Walter Blondin, Colette Poitras, Leanne Goose,
George Blondin. Raymond Yakeleya, Antoine Mountain
Editors: Sarah Stewart & Raymond Yakeleya
Artists: Antoine Mountain, Ruth Schefter, Deborah Desmarais
978-1-988824-63-5 *(pbk)* | 978-1-988824-74-1 *(audiobook)*
978-1-988824-75-8 *(e-book)*

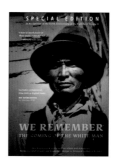

Stories of Métis Women: Tales My Kookum Told Me
Authors/Editors: Bailey Oster & Marilyn Lizee
Foreword: Audrey Poitras

978-1-988824-21-5 *(pbk)* | 978-1-988824-69-7 *(audiobook)*
978-1-98882-46-8-0 *(e-book)*

Siksikaitsitapi: Stories of the Blackfoot People
Authors: Payne Many Guns, Crystal Many Fingers,
Sheena Potts, Latasha Calf Robe, Tim Fox,
Marlene Yellow Horn, DerRic Starlight
Foreword: Alayna Many Guns
978-1-988824-83-3 *(pbk)* | 978-1-988824-89-5 *(audio)*
978-1-988824-88-8 *(e-book)*

Why RU Still Here? A Lillian Mystery
Lynda Partridge
Illustrations: Dave Nicholson

978-1-988824-82-6 *(pbk)* | 978-1-988824-93-2 *(audio)*
978-1-988824-92-5 *(e-book)*